Cookie Rescue

By Susan Ring
Illustrated by Alan Batson

DISNEY PRESS

NEW YORK

 PRESS

First Edition
Library of Congress Cataloging-in-Publication Data on file
ISBN 978-1-4231-1026-2

For more Disney Press fun, visit www.disneybooks.com

The  is out in Sheet Rock Hills.

sun

Manny takes the tools for a ride.

Look! Here comes Mrs. Portillo.
She runs over to the .
truck
Maybe she has some of her
yummy .
cookies

"I don't smell any [cookies]," says [Dusty].

Mrs. Portillo can't bake cookies for

the town's Best Baker contest.

She needs help with her new [oven].

Manny

and the tools will help.
They will move her new oven

into her  .

house

*Uno…dos…tres…cuatro…cinco
…seis…siete…*
Let's get to work!

Oh, no! The oven does not fit.

It is too big for the  door.

How will Mrs. Portillo

bake cookies for

the contest?

"I will tap it in," says .

Pat

"I will cut the door," says .

Dusty

No, no. That won't work!

Here comes Mr. Lopart and Fluffy.

Fluffy really wants to say hello!

Oh, no!  is afraid of Fluffy.

Rusty

Rusty runs to the backyard.

Thump!

Rusty runs into the back  .

Fluffy makes sure that Rusty is okay.

Stretch has a good idea!

They will take down the big door.

The oven will fit now.

The new  is in the house.
oven

Mrs. Portillo can bake her !
cookies

Here comes .
Mrs. Portillo

Does she need more help?

No. She has ![cookies] for everyone!
cookies

Yummy!